Summer in Gree

Cricket and Coconut Cake

Vanessa Webbe

Webbewrite Publication

Easy Reading paperbacks and ebooks for Young Readers

Cricket and Coconut Cake

A product of Webbewrite Publication
Webbes Ground, Gingerland, Nevis
ISBN: 978-976-96288-8-5
Registered with CARICOM

Author Contact: webbev3@hotmail.com

Major Illustrations by Arcquela Bendeito

The children living in Green Garden love to play with each other.

They love to play cricket. It is another bright sunny day and they are ready to play.

"Let us play a game of cricket together," Sam called out to everyone.

"Harry, can you get the bat?"

"I will get the ball," said Sam.

"Jerry and Sally will run after the ball," exclaimed Sam.

"Ruff! Ruff!" Spike barked aloud.

"Ok, yes, you can also play, Spike."

"You can run and get the ball, too."

Sam bowled the ball to Harry.

Harry hit the ball hard.

It was a hard knock for four runs.

The ball fell into Mrs. Hanley's flower garden.

Will they get the ball back?

The children cheered for Harry.

Mrs. Hanley was clapping too.

She enjoyed watching the children playing cricket.

She will always throw the ball, back over the fence.

The children will shout, “Thank you, Mrs. Hanley.”

“Play on,” Mrs. Hanley will say cheerfully.

“You may play on the West Indies cricket team one day,”

she encouraged the children.

She is a very kind neighbour.

"That was good batting, Harry. Now, let's give Jerry a chance to bat as well. We will all get a turn to bat," Sam assured everyone.

With a bright smile on his face, Jerry ran to get the bat. He was excited to get a chance to bat.

"I will hit the ball very hard!" Jerry bragged.

"We will see," replied Sam, just before bowling the ball to Jerry.

Jerry hit the ball up in the air. Sam ran to catch it.

The ball bounced on the ground before he could do so and rolled away. Jerry started running with the bat in his hand, to get runs.

Harry chased after the ball.

“One run,” Jerry shouted, waving the bat in the air, as he came back to the cricket crease.

“I will run for two,” he teased and started running again.

Just then, Harry picked up the ball and threw it to Sally, who hit the stump, before Jerry could get back. Sally had run out Jerry for one run.

Sam, Sally and Harry were all cheering for the run-out dismissal.

Jerry walked away from the wicket, not as cheerful but hopeful.

“Next time, it won’t be that easy for you to get me out,” Jerry told his friends, as he handed over the bat.

The children could hear Mrs. Hanley clapping

and cheering them on, from her fence.

It was Sam's turn to bat.

Sally now had a turn to bowl the ball.

Sam hit the ball high in the air.

It was a hard hit for six runs.

Oh, no! The ball landed in Mr. Brown's Garden.

Will the children get back the ball?

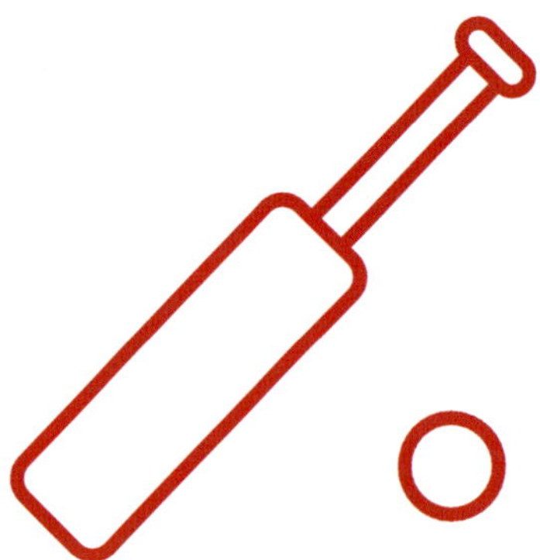

The children had a frown on their faces.

Mr. Brown would not want anyone to come near his garden of vegetables.

Besides, he has a big, brown guard dog.

How will they get the ball again?

Mr. Brown came out of his house.

"You boy for Mrs. Millie, stop hitting your ball over my fence!" Mr. Brown shouted out, as he pointed to Sam, who was holding the bat in his hand.

"Sorry, Mr. Brown!" Sam shouted back respectfully, for Mr. Brown to hear his voice.

"May we please have the ball back?" Sam asked politely.

"No, of course not," Mr. Brown replied.

"You will hit the ball over my fence again."

"Besides, I am very busy right now."

The children were very sad.

“Sally, please use your crying voice to ask Mr. Brown to throw the ball back to us,” Sam urged his sister.

“That’s a very good idea,” said Harry.

“Ok, I will try my best,” agreed Sally.

She started to rob her eyes with her hands as if to let Mr. Brown think that she was crying then in a sulking voice she said, “Hello, Mr. Brown. Please, please, may we, may we have the ball back?”

The children felt that Mr. Brown was sure to feel sorry for Sally.

“Not a chance,” came the reply from Mr. Brown. Sorry but I can’t help you right now. If I leave off what I am doing to throw the ball back each time, I will not get anything done. Later, I will give it to your mother, Mrs. Millie. She will give it to you.”

“Well let’s call it off today,” said Sam sighing. “If Sally’s crying voice cannot help us to get the ball back, then I don’t know what will. Mr. Brown needs to be a bit more kind.”

They started removing the stumps, in the dirt road, that was seldom traversed by vehicles, as it was at the end of the main road in the village, an area that had become their play field. How disappointed they were, now that their game of cricket was disrupted, not by rain as sometimes happened, but by Mr. Brown, who seemed not to care about the children having fun in the village.

The children bowed their heads as they were getting ready to clear the field, when they heard a voice say, “Don’t worry, children, you will get back your ball.” It was Mrs. Hanley, who had heard the entire conversation and wanted to help the children.

“I know just what to take to Mr. Brown, so you can get back your ball,” Mrs. Hanley said confidently to the children.

“He is just a bit lonely and a little cranky, but he still has a good heart,” Mrs. Hanley told the children.

Mrs. Hanley soon walked over to Mr. Brown's house

with a paper bag in her hand. The children saw her talking to Mr. Brown.

Then surprisingly, the children saw Mr. Brown smiling.

Next, he picked up the ball to throw it over the fence.

His dog gave out a loud "ruff, ruff, ruff", wagging its tail, as if he was happy for the children, when Mr. Brown picked up the ball.

"You, boy for Mrs. Millie, catch the ball!" he shouted out.

Sam tried catching the ball, but it slipped through his hands and fell to the ground.

"Thank, you Mr. Brown," Sam replied gratefully, with a broad smile on his face.

Spike ran after the ball. Spike picked up the ball with his mouth and carried it to Sally, to bowl again. The children gave Spike a round of applause for fielding so well. “Hurray Spike!” they applauded.

Then the children heard clapping on the other side of the fence.

It was both Mrs. Millie and Mr. Brown clapping, this time.

"You are playing a fun game of cricket," said Mr. Brown to the children.

Then he came closer to the fence.

"I used to play cricket, too," Mr. Brown confessed to the children.

Mrs. Hanley came back to her fence to watch the game.

Sam was very curious to know what was in the paper bag that Mrs. Hanley had carried for Mr. Brown, that made him smile and throw the ball over the fence so quickly. But he did not want to ask from so far away.

Sam called Sally to take the bat.

“It is your turn to bat, Sally,” Sam informed his sister.

Sally passed the ball on to Harry and took the bat.

Sam positioned himself close to Mrs. Hanley's fence to field the ball.

"Thank you for getting the ball for us Mrs. Hanley. But I am just curious to know. Please can you tell us what was in the bag that made Mr. Brown smile like that?"

Mrs. Hanley laughed out.

"Oh, it was just a large slice of coconut cake. Mr. Brown loves coconut cake. I made some yesterday," Mrs. Hanley replied, still laughing.

"Oh, my mother makes good coconut cake, too. We call them coconut drops. I will ask my mother to make a few drops for Mr. Brown." said Sam to Mrs. Hanley.

"You are right, Mrs. Hanley!" added Sam, "Mr. Brown is not that bad.

He is just a little lonely. He was very happy to see you.

We will ask our parents to visit him and take

coconut cake for him, now and then."

"We want all the neighbours to help us to get the ball back so that we can keep playing cricket, on our street," Sam reasoned.

"We all have to get along really well,

like our Sunday School teacher said we should. But also, for the sake of cricket," Sam stated.

Just then, Sally hit the ball high in the air.

Harry ran after the ball, to catch it. Then he stretched out his hands and caught the ball.

"I got it!" Harry bellowed out.

"Good catch, you boy for Mrs. Jones," Mr. Brown exclaimed over his fence, pointing to Harry.

"You children are very good at cricket. You can make it on the West Indies cricket team," Mr. Brown commended, clapping his hands.

"Wow, that slice of coconut cake must have been very delicious," Sam whispered to Mrs. Hanley, drawing closer to the fence. For Sam, Mr. Brown's face was now beaming with smiles, as bright as the sun that was giving off golden rays, while they were playing cricket.

"Well, after the game, I will pass a slice of coconut cake over the fence to each of you and some water as well. You do need to drink more water while playing cricket in the hot sun. Lovely weather for cricket though," remarked Mrs. Hanley.

“We will break now guys,” Sam called out to everyone.

“Let us take a tea break for some coconut cake and water from Mrs. Hanley.”

“Her coconut cake made Mr. Brown smile and throw the ball back to us. It ought to make us play better cricket, too.”

Everyone, walked over to the fence gleefully, to get a slice of coconut cake from Mrs. Hanley.

“Do you really think we can one day play for the West Indies cricket team?” Sam asked Mrs. Hanley.

“Of course, you can,” replied Mrs. Hanley. Many Nevisians have played for the West Indies cricket team and you can one day too. I am certain that many cricketers who have played for the West Indies team started just like you, playing cricket in the street. You are the best little cricketers I know,” Mrs. Hanley told the children. “You keep playing and I will keep baking coconut cake for tea break.”

"Thank you, Mrs. Hanley," the children replied. Spike was also given a piece of cake to eat and gave a 'thank you' bark. The children gobbled down the coconut cake, making sounds to let Mrs. Hanley know how much they enjoyed eating her cake. Then they quickly drank the water and hurried back to the street, to continue their game of cricket.

The End

Thank you to our sponsor.

ABOUT THE AUTHOR

Vanessa Webbe grew up in Cox Village, Nevis in an extended family with her grandfather Daniel Webbe, mother Bernadine Webbe, siblings, and cousins. She has many fond memories of her childhood days, especially listening to her grandfather telling stories. She is thankful for her God given gift to express herself in writing and to have the opportunity to share stories with children through her writing. As an author, her genre includes faith based and children literature. Through her writing, she especially enjoys creating a happy reading world for children. Ms. Webbe now lives in Webbes Ground, Gingerland. She is a mother of two grown children Kadeise and Kleeton Hendrickson and grandmother of four adorable grandchildren. She enjoys baking, gardening and sharing her Christian faith with others.

CRICKET AND COCUNUT CAKE

Made in the USA
Middletown, DE
11 April 2023